First published in 2017
by Anthony Bogrjantseff

Copyright © 2017 Anthony Bogrjantseff

The right of Anthony Bogrjantseff to be identified as the author of this work has been asserted in accordance with §77 and §78 of the Copyright Design and Patterns Act 1988.

All right reserved. No part of this publication may be reproduced, stored in a retrieval system, or transmitted in any from or by any means, electronic, mechanical, photocopying, recording, or otherwise, without the prior written permission of the author.

Cover image by Anthony Bogrjantseff

Design by Anthony Bogrjantseff

The Tales of a Stone Lion

Also from Anthony Bogrjantseff:

"Talking to a Shaman"

Please follow the author's blog:
http://www.facebook.com/talkingtoashaman

An autumn leaf is falling from the branch of a maple tree. Where is it flying, across the water of my pond? I love to sit and watch it flying. A maple born and gone with the wind...

I am sitting on a chair with a mug of coffee in my hand. I am drinking coffee, the leaf is drifting away, I have seen this many times before...

Anthony Bogrjantseff

The Tales of a Stone Lion

Foreword

Almost every person in the world had heard about London, and most of those who have visited London or live in the city have been to one of its biggest museums, the

British Museum. It is a grandiose building in central London, located between four short streets that can be easily walked. Starting clockwise from Montague Place you will pass through Montague Street, Great Russell Street, and Bloomsbury Street that change into Bedford Square half way through your walk. Soon you find yourself at Montague Place again, where we meet the main star of these stories.

If you have visited the museum, most likely you have walked through the main gates on the Great Russell Street and have seen the lions carved out of stone guarding the gates. Most people do so. However, not many have thought of peeking behind the museum's building, and onto Montague Place. This small street is not too busy during the day apart from a few school coaches bringing the students into the museum, and the street is practically deserted in the evening with not a soul around after ten pm.

There seems to be nothing of interest there, except for two stone lions looking exactly like those at the building façade. Yet, this similarity is an illusion. There is a lot of action happening at the back gate, invisible and unknown to the passers-by. Only the selected few know the secret of one of these lions at the back gates. In fact, I might be the only one to know that one of these lions is not merely a stone sculpture, and there is life burning inside one of the lions, this stone sculpture is, and has been, alive for many decades...

Once upon a time, many years ago, a small flock of fairies from the Kensington Gardens flew above the British Museum grounds. One of the fairies felt tired and decided to have some rest. She flew to the back gates of the museum and perched on the tip of the nose of one of the lions. After the fairy felt strong enough to fly she joined her little sisters, but when she flew off the lion's nose a few specks of the golden dust fell off her wings and landed on the lion's nose. Those were not just any specks; they were magic fairy dust which gave life to the stone lion on the right side of the back gates.

Since then, the lion came alive inside his heavy stone frame, unable to move but able to think and feel, observe and remember the life that flows around him like a river. It may be somebody else's life, not his own, but, nonetheless, it is still very exciting and fascinating. His entire life this stone lion had wanted to be able to move, to leave his pedestal, to walk around, to roar. But all he can do is to sit motionless and observe, think, and remember what he had seen... Being a not an ordinary statue, the Stone Lion can speak with other magical creatures, and I will share with you some of his stories.

More than anything in the world, the Stone Lion loves the rain. According to his own words, it was raining when he was born. He doesn't know how many times he had seen the rain during his long life as a museum gates' guard, but every time it rains he feels happy enjoying every raindrop. It's not surprising then, that the first tale he shared with me was about the rain.

Tale One

The rain and the water drops

The raindrops falling from the sky in a hot summer evening do not die crashing against the concrete pavement, although it may look like this from the first glance. Oh, no! The raindrops are tirelessly seeking every smallest crack and cavity in the pavement, trickling onto the road, seeping through in between the cobblestones...

The water wants to infiltrate the ground and continue its way forward, now hidden from the human eye. The water knows that even the tiniest water drop is important and makes a difference. Just one extra droplet of water may set off the burst of a mountain lake. The flooded lake will give water to the dried up bushes and saturate the soil. The bushes will come alive and produce the berries and the sprigs that will feed the birds and animals.

Just a single water drop may be all that is needed to provide water to a tree imprisoned in the hot concrete jungle of the city. An old tree will grow green again, and the birds will build nests in its crown, to make safe home for their little chicks. The water never stops moving, and every raindrop is priceless. I wish that people also understood the cost of their actions and words.

Tale two

A single day, the whole life

My whole world consists of the short section of the street visible to my eyes. Remember, I cannot even turn my head or move my eyes to see any further than the end of my street. The only life I see is the one going in front of my eyes, and a bit from my peripheral vision. Thousands of pedestrians walk, run, and jog past me sitting on this pedestal. This street is only one of many walks that they take. It probably is not their favourite walk either, not the most picturesque, and not the longest. But this is all I have. It is not likely that I will ever see anything else.

One rainy day for a human is just that – one day of a bad weather. One day from their whole life. But for many other creatures one day is their whole life. In human terms, some insects only live one day. But for those insects the day is long. If the weather is bad on that day so it is, they will never see the good weather and won't know what the sunshine is like.

The value of an event depends on your perception. It should never be forgotten that a minor episode in *your* life may have a lasting consequence on *somebody else's* future.

Tale Three

Two courteous gentlemen

It happened many years ago, back in the days when people thought that I was already ancient. But that was a human perception and I thought of myself as very young indeed. However, this story is not about me.

This is about two mature gentlemen who both had rather a venerable appearance. Over a half a dozen years, these gentlemen were walking this street passing me on the way. They passed me and my gates at the same time, one gentleman walking from the left and another from the right hand side. This was in the mornings. In the evenings, they passed me on exactly the same spot at in reverse. Twice a day I saw them almost simultaneously walking on my street and meeting right in front of me. The first time they passed one another they didn't pay any attention to each other. After a few days their eyes began to meet, and after some more time meeting like that they began to nod to each other acknowledging each other's presence. After about a year, these gentlemen have developed a kind of greeting ritual – their eyes would meet, they exchange the nods; slow down their walking and finishing with lifting up their hats. Sometime they might share a half-smile but never exchanged a single word or a handshake.

This continued for many years, and once this ritual was disturbed.

When the gentleman who usually entered the street on my right hand side did not appear in the morning, his counterpart looked somewhat perplexed and confused. The routine was broken. He stopped in the middle of the street right in front of me, he looked totally bewildered and searched with his eyes the crowd of pedestrians hurrying by, hoping to see his acquaintance. This continued for a few moments...then the other gentleman finally appeared at the opposite end of the street. Everything suddenly fell into place. They both continued towards each other and exchanged their usual morning niceties.

The relief on the face of the first gentleman was indescribable! You can rarely see someone glowing with such a joy as the first gentleman's face when he saw his friend walking up to him. Since then, their ritual was never disturbed. For many more years they were meeting on my street – twice a day on weekdays and once a day on weekends.

Isn't it amazing? Sometimes, you never share a word with a person, yet they enter your life and embed themselves in there so firmly that you cannot even fathom they can suddenly disappear. They become an integral part of your life. This incident had demonstrated there are no unimportant people in the human life. Everyone is priceless, it's just some people spend more time with you and are more involved, when others are simply there. Take away one ingredient from our established routine and our life seems shaken.

Tale Four

The people who complain

Sometimes, when people get tired walking around the city they need some rest. Many of the passers-by obviously thought my pedestal is a great place to get some rest from the sightseeing. They would sit in the shadow of my cold stone body at the bottom of the plinth, leaning their backs against the coolness of the stone. Some people climb up and sit on the plinth. Some just sit on the ground near the plinth. Occasionally, someone starts complaining about their life aloud. Do they talk to me or to themselves? I don't know, but I am a good listener. If they talk to me, it must be there is nobody else they can moan to, nobody else to share their complaints with.

I do wonder though, why moan to me? It's not like I can do anything to help, I cannot even nod in acknowledgement!

But I patiently listen, not without interest. Each time a person would start moaning I want to say – stop! Look at yourself – unlike me, you have the opportunities to change your life. I don't. Unlike me, you have arms and legs that move, a tongue that you can use, a language that is understood by others. I don't. You complain about your life to *me*, when it should be me complaining to *you*. Unlike you, all I have is my thoughts locked inside this stone body. I cannot even open my mouth and speak to you, the people. The only living things that understand my speaking are the magical creatures – the Kensington Fairy, and the Black Raven from the Tower of London. I don't even know whether they can be called 'living' because they can't speak with you, the people, either.

I sit here motionless for decades, and while I could be complaining about this to you, instead, I offer you the shade and a listening ear. Because there is no point in complaining if you can't, or won't, do anything about your complaint.

Tale Five

The fairy's wings and people's dreams

It was a dark and quiet night when my little friend, the Kensington Fairy, came to visit me.

"Aren't you lucky, you have the wings, you can fly. These people I see every day don't have wings, no flying for them", - I said to her.

She responded passionately:

"The wings for flying are not *that* important! What is important is that people have dreams. People's fantasies, their aspirations – they are people's wings. Those who know how to use their dreams, they can fly too!"

Of course, the Fairy was talking metaphorically about people flying; even I could understand that despite not being able to even walk.

"The dreams will support them in rising higher to the clouds and above. People's dreams are their wings", - continued the Kensington Fairy. – "Sadly, some people don't know how to use the power of their dreams to turn them into wings, so for them the dreams are just a nuisance. Some people can dream but do nothing about their dreams, without any action they cannot rise above the ordinary, above their own heads, let alone above the clouds. These people are like small baby birds – the little chicks have wings like a grown up bird has, but the little ones cannot fly yet because they haven't learned, because their wings are not yet fully developed and not strong enough. Some people only have dreams but take no action to achieve them, so their dreams are small and weak like the little bird's wings."

The Fairy had a lot to say on the wings and dreams subject:

"Being able to hope, to desire something, to dream big, to have a goal and aim to achieve it – this is a very valuable characteristic of a human but it needs continuing nurture and development. An ability to have ambitions, to aspire for a better future makes people different from other creatures of this world. It should become a norm for people to pursue their dreams, like for the birds it normal to use their wings for flying. I sometime wish I had dreams instead of my wings", - concluded the Fairy wistfully, and I would second that.

Tale Six

Rich boy, poor boy

In those days when the phones began to appear in the homes of the London residents, young students used to gather together on the steps of my pedestal. They were playing, chatting, doing their homework and explaining to each other some of the topics covered during the school classes.

Among these students there was a boy dressed up a little better than the rest of the group. He was very boisterous and always participating in the boys' games, presenting himself as a leader. It was evident that he thought himself better than the others as he would often talk down to his mates. He didn't take any interest in conversations about learning and only joined in on the school topics when he wanted to borrow somebody's work to copy.

One other student in this group was the opposite of this wealthy boy. This student often looked scruffy. It was obvious his family wasn't wealthy because some of the boy's clothes didn't fit him well and looked as they were handed down to him second-hand, perhaps by his older brother. This boy wasn't very keen in playing the active games and didn't engage in the natter too much. He just came along with the rest of the boys and then sat down on the stone and read his books.

I observed this group over the years, as the boys were growing and maturing. Some years later they were no longer boys but the young men. They still maintained their odd friendship and continued coming to meet up by my pedestal, although not regularly now. I was unable to work out now who is who, because there were less people in their group. Listening to the conversations, I understood the wealthy boy was kicked out of school and went uneducated and joined his parent's business. He wasted his youth, and wasted his parent's wealth gradually ruining the business. The young man who used to be a boy from the poor family had graduated with good grades and continued higher education; he now had a good job and dressed smartly.

The tables have turned. As it often happens, those with limited opportunities are determined to succeed and work for it, against the odds achieving more than was expected of them. Yet, those who have many chances to succeed but no desire to put any work in end up a failure.

Tale Seven

The secret of a soul

I have not been inside the museum myself. My place is on the outside, guarding the back gates. But I often overhear the museum visitors discussing what they have seen inside. Do they see a lot, indeed! There are paintings, there are sculptures, and there are artefacts. I have overheard there are also exhibitions being held at the museum showing different exhibits. Apparently, there is some kind of storage somewhere in the museum where more artefacts are being kept because there is not enough room in the museum halls to show them. So, the organisers sometime swap some exhibits for others taking them out from the vaults. I also heard there are exhibits held of the items that are given on loan, that don't actually belong to the museum but maybe to a private person, or to another museum. I don't know much about what's there, you see – I have never been inside. I can only build an imaginary picture in my head from what I have heard, so please excuse me if I get things wrong at times.

So, I have heard from the group of foreign visitors there was a statue of an ancient god. I have learnt there are many more other stone statues inside the museum. People usually ignore the details, they just look at the statue, learn what it is, and continue on their way. Other people may stop and discuss the statue, its features. Some people may discuss their private things instead, standing next to the statue.

People feel safe doing all that. The stone statue may be shaped as a human but it isn't a human. It can't overhear them. The statue is just a statue, right? Wrong. Who knows, if any of them are alive, like me?

No one knows whether a statue can hide a living soul, except me of course! Breaking up the stone statue won't help to look inside it and see if it has a soul. The soul is invisible. Equally, it would be very naïve to think we can read another person's soul simply by looking into their eyes or by talking to them. The human soul is a mystery and is sacred; no one knows what another person's soul can hide. The human soul can be like a fresh field full of fragrant bright and beautiful flowers, on another hand it can be like a burnt out field of dead crops.

Tale Eight

The spirit of a childhood

I have been guarding the gates of the British Museum for many years. The pedestrians usually don't even notice me, and those who do still don't realise that I can see and hear them. This is very interesting, because people typically assume that nobody is watching if there are no other people around, and so they behave whichever way they wish. The statue of a stone lion doesn't count, they reckon. It is only a statue. But is it?

I have been observing people with much curiosity. When they think they are on their own and nobody can see them, people's behaviour can change. In old days, even the most respectable gentlemen allowed themselves some boisterous tricks – they would change their steady walk and may start hopping on one foot. Some may walk with a dance. Maybe they were listening to music only heard by them. Some very presentable looking men would do something childish and unexpected of them, when they think they are totally alone. But even though their actions were mischievous they were totally harmless.

This has changed in the recent years. People often walk looking down to the pavement, or without taking their eyes from the screen of a small device they are holding in their hands. Mobile phones. Smart phones. No silly behaviour anymore. And strangely enough, people no longer care whether they are being seen or heard by anyone. They speak loudly with no consideration if anyone can overhear them. People have become quite indifferent to whether they are surrounded by other people or not. They walk straight ahead without looking up from the small screen, not worrying if they will walk into another person. This made me think, do these electronic devices matter more than people? Where is the spirit of a childhood?

Tale Nine

The spider web

Practically on any street in any city in the world there are hardworking, but not very obvious inhabitants. There are many of them also living on my street. They don't normally catch the eye of the passers-by, and they are not trying to attract attention to themselves. But, if a pedestrian would notice them, he would rarely take any interest in these creatures' handiwork. You might have guessed I am talking about spiders. The spiders live everywhere. The spider webs can be found anywhere. Sometimes they go unnoticed because they are almost invisible. The spiders have mastered a skill of hiding and blending in with the surroundings. But the spiders' crafting skill is even more amazing than their talent of disguise. The exquisite webs are being knitted from a single point; the spider works around in a circle and creates a beautiful net with a very neat and geometrically perfect motif, where all threads are passing through the perimeter. Seemingly simple, the spider webs are extremely complex with their fragile threads crisscrossing and hanging in mid-air. The finest weave of the finest fibers, the web is woven with great tenacity and grace. Multiple invisible yarns knitted by an invisible weaver. These spider webs are mesmerizing, yet real.

I reckon they resemble the human life – a web of hundreds of various routes leading to different opportunities, all joined together. More often than not, these routes are invisible, but that doesn't make them less real, and each route can bring about many different outcomes, each outcome depending not so much on the web pattern of the human life, but on the avenue a man will choose to follow.

Tale Ten

The drinking bird

One early morning when the sun had only just risen above the horizon but the streets were still deserted, a little bird sat down near my plinth. There were no cars on the street yet, no pedestrians. There was no usual city noise, just the stillness of a sunny peaceful morning.

The bird did not come without a reason. The concrete near my pedestal is broken, it has a cavity that collects water after the rain, and the water remains there for a long time. In the shade of the large crowns of the old trees and in the shadow of my body most of the time, the water remains quite cold and clean. It rained the night before this morning, and the bird came to have a drink. The bird had flown around me for a while then it sat near the little puddle, closed its wings and walked towards the water. When the bird got to the paddle it tilted its head and stood still looking at the water. I guessed the bird wasn't just looking at the water, but was examining its own reflection in the water surface. After a long look, the bird poked its beak into the water and the reflection disappeared. Having had a drink, the bird immediately flew away.

Once the water had settled in the puddle, it was my turn to look at my own reflection in it. I didn't see much as I cannot bend my head as the living animal. But what I saw was illuminating. I understood that my reflection, be it in the puddle of water or in the window of the bus driving past me, is only a reflection of my image but not a reflection of *me*. It doesn't define me other than by resembling my appearance.

The reflection is only a reflection; it doesn't carry the same identity as the real thing. Look at your own reflection in the water mirror. When you disturb the water glaze, your reflection will disappear but you will not. Have a look at your reflection in the bus window while standing at the bus stop. Don't board the bus but wait till it drives off – and your reflection in the bus windows will slide off, but you – you will remain. Your reflection is merely an image of you but has no substance, just like your shadow has no depth.

Tale Eleven

The real value of money

I remember one boy who frequently ran on my street. I remember this boy because there was something special about him. Every time, regardless of the speed he was running at, the boy was carefully observing the ground under his feet and stopped and picked every coin he noticed. Even the small and rusted copper penny would not escape his attention. Indeed, he was picking up the coins that others would not even count as money. But he was persistent and every time he found a small change on the road, his face would light up with satisfaction of a discoverer. I don't know whether he was so poor and needed every penny he found, or whether he had enjoyed the thrill of 'treasure hunting' – the excitement of finding what he was looking for.

I observed this boy for a while, and it became clear to me that happiness cannot be measured; it is different for everyone. Some may wait their whole life for something big to happen to make them happy, while others, like this boy, can find joy in small things every day.

The fog

When the cold wind is blowing from the South, and the seagulls fly over from the river Thames and you can hear their piercing cries above your head, it is at this time the London fog seems especially ominous. My loyal little friend, the Kensington Fairy, says that such nights are particularly scary in the Kensington Gardens.

During the dark hours of the night, the fairies are petrified of the menacing fog creeping through the city and to reassure each other and to keep safe, all fairies gather together and hide in the center of one of the large flowers growing in the gardens. All the flowers go to sleep at night and close up their buds, but the fairies wake up the flower and, when the petals open, the fairies find refuge in the middle. Each night the fairies choose a different flower with large petals that can shield them from the chilly night. This way the fairies feel protected by the warm embrace of another living creature and sheltered from the frosty and frightening London fog. The fairies spend the whole night inside the flower bud cuddled together, grateful for this sanctuary.

During the night, the fog rises from the water getting thicker and whiter so that you cannot see anything closer than two feet. The air becomes murky, and this cloudy milky substance is hovering just above the ground, moving slightly and rising higher, changing its shape, as if it is looking around where to go next. The fog is now thick and very cold; it begins its travel through the London streets and along the river banks. It floods the parks and courtyards; it spills its icy touch over the shipyards and wharfs. The maze of the small streets and mews in Holborn is now swathed in this white thick mist surrounding the buildings and creeping near to my stone paws, trying to touch them...

I don't feel the cold. I am made out of stone. But I can understand the feeling. The night is quiet. The fog is now lying all over the city like a blanket, like wet cotton wool, silencing all the city sounds, obscuring the views, distorting the images and swallowing up the living world. The life comes to a standstill during this time until the first rays of sunshine pierce this thick haze sending the fog away. Only I, and the other lions, sit still guarding the museum gates, come day or night.

Tale Twelve

The crowd

It is windy today. The wind blows quietly, moving the dust and grains of the sand along the pavement of my street, and they roll closer to my feet and stay there... I want to touch the sand. I want put my paw on the sand and feel it between my toes. But I cannot do that, of course. Because I am made of stone and I cannot move.

But I know that if I could pick these sand particles they will all look the same, totally devoid of any personality. They are not living creatures; they are simply the material that the stone is made of. But my stone statue has life in it – mine. So, maybe, the grains of sand have life in them too? Sometime, when the wind is strong it lifts the sand off the ground and tiny sand particles land on the top of my nose. I can see them closely and, indeed, they are not all the same at all – they are different in shape, size, colour, texture, weight, composition.

I have seen many people and can say that people in the crowd look all the same. It's a living, breathing, moving mass that has no faces. But when you look beyond the crowd and see each individual separately, when you watch them communicating one-on-one, it becomes obvious they are very different. Some are intelligent, others are not so much. Some are happy, but others are not. The most amazing fact is that while each person is extraordinary, the crowd swallows them and they lose their uniqueness and become a faceless and meaningless particle in this sea of people.

Tale Thirteen

The change

Everything in the universe is in motion. Even I am in motion, because my mind is not permanently attached to the stone pedestal on which I sit. While this pedestal supports my heavy and motionless body, it does not restrict the flow of my thoughts.

The pedestrians walk past me, the seasons come and go, and before you know it the decades are gone.

I am still here as I was before, but my mind follows the people, the seasons, the years. It is not possible to live without changing, even if you are a stone lion. My mind and my soul change as the years go by, while my body is practically the same as before, except for wearing away from the harsh weather. It is possible to remain the same on the outside and be different on the inside, because your body is only a vessel for your mind and soul.

People are obsessed with the outside, with the way they look. But very often, the human body is quite deceptive and the beautiful exterior is only a container concealing a grey soul and an empty mind. This happens when a person is too concerned about their physical appearance and neglects his soul, so all that remains is a superficial shell with no substance.

Tale Fourteen

The bench

It was some time ago, a young man had started to come to the back gate of the museum every day. He didn't go inside the museum but always sat on the bench near my stone pedestal. Every time he had a thick book with him and he would settle comfortably and read his book. He did nothing else, just sat there and read for a couple of hours. He would appear early evening without fail, arriving around six and leaving at about eight o'clock or so. He had somewhat a sad expression on his face.

Then, around mid-June, a young lady started to come to the same bench. She would come around four in the afternoon and leave just a few minutes before her place was taken by the young man I already got acquainted with. She also sat there reading her book and did nothing else. She too, appeared upset about something all the time. I noticed that her book cover looked the same as the young man's so I reckon it must have been exactly the same story they were reading. Possibly, the story in the book was so sad that they both were getting upset by reading it? I do not know.

This continued every day for a few months – the young man and the lady sat on the same bench in exactly the same spot, reading the same book and yet they have never met.

But one day, this young man came to the bench half an hour earlier than usual and found his favourite place taken by this young lady, reading the same book! The sad expression on his face had changed to a bemused one first, then he smiled and the girl returned his smile. From then on, he always tried to arrive half an hour earlier, and the girl was no longer in a hurry to go home.

By observing them, I reasoned that everything in this world is twofold. If there is one lonely person somewhere, then there is another equally lonely person somewhere else too. Or, there might be two lonely people in exactly the same place but at the wrong time. The destiny's challenge is to help the two lonely people meet.

Tale Fifteen

Time control

Time is valuable. Time is irreplaceable. Time is something I have plenty of.

When I look at young children walking with their parents holding their hands, I understand what differentiates the little ones from the grown-ups. The children have all the time in the world ahead of them, while the adults have already used some, or most, of their time.

The older people get, the faster their time goes. With maturity comes experience, but it takes away your time. Mature people are conscious of this lack of time and try to catch up on the time lost, to regain control over it. Controlling time is hard; it requires a lot of work, a lot of effort. While the children play the time slows down for them, one week can feel like a long time. But for their parents, the time just flies and before they know the whole year is gone. In an attempt to catch up they are always in a rush, always hurry up. They always need to be somewhere. Paradoxically, the more they hurry the less they succeed.

– How do you control the time? – You may ask. But I cannot answer this question. Yes, I am old. And yes, I do have a lot of time like the children, despite being old. But I am not a human, so the time has a different meaning for me. I know one thing though – trying to catch up with time is initially a hopeless and useless task. Therefore, you should try not to waste it in the first place.

Tale Sixteen

The Black Raven

I am a stone lion and I cannot move, but I still can make friends. Remember the Kensington Fairy? She is a good friend to me. I am also lucky to have another friend. This friend, too, is magical. And while the fairy is a young creature, this other friend is very, very old. I am not certain if he is older than me, but I reckon, he must be one of the oldest residents of London, perhaps preceding the time of the Tower of London ghosts. At least, he tells me that he lived in this area even before the construction of the Tower of London.

This friend is a Black Raven. Of course, I know the raven's life doesn't span several centuries. But my friend is not an ordinary bird, he is magical, so the time as we understand it doesn't apply to him.

The Black Raven doesn't visit me as often as the Kensington Fairy. I only see him infrequently, perhaps every few years. But this does not make our encounters less desirable and his visits are never boring.

This can only happen with true friends – you may not see them for a long time, you may not even communicate at all for a while. Yet, when you do meet and catch up, you will feel as you have never been apart. This is because true friends always have their place in your heart, which means they have never left you and you have never left them.

Tale Seventeen

True friends

Very often, particularly during the period from autumn to spring, when the evenings begin early and the nights are long, I have many visitors. The strangers just stop by and start a conversation, or, rather, a monologue. You, of course, remember that I cannot respond but only listen. It doesn't stop people talking to me anyway, and they talk to me as if I could. These people must be in a desperate need to offload their thoughts and feelings to someone, and it doesn't matter if they don't get a single word in response. It what they say that counts.

The longest and most detailed monologue I have heard had lasted over an hour, despite that it was raining heavily. A well-dressed woman walked towards me and looked straight into my face. I don't know whether she realised that I was actually listening and could see her. She stood in front of me, hiding from the rain under a huge umbrella, telling me what had been bothering her. I learned that she is a successful business woman responsible for the work of many people. I won't bore you with all her troubles, but she talked and talked. Her story was full of emotions filled with worry, uncertainty, sadness and anger. At the end of her monologue she just burst into tears, and then walked off.

So, here I sit and listen to everyone who wants to talk to me and wonder – why can't people find a listener better than a stone lion? Someone to listen to their troubles, another person? Perhaps they cannot trust other people with their secrets? It appears that some people cannot find a companionship with others because from their stories I have learnt they are surrounded by the people who are insensitive. Where is this world going if a stone lion can find friends, yet the people can't?

Tale Eighteen

A gentleman and his hat

The story I want to tell you had happened a very long time ago, back in the days when it was customary for all gentlemen to wear hats.

That day was particularly windy and there were not too many pedestrians passing me on the street. Maybe the harsh weather had scared them away. Even those that did brave the weather were in a hurry to escape the fierce wind and get indoors.

Then I saw him. The gentlemen stood out from the crowd. Maybe, because I have not seen him before. Maybe, because his stance was different from the others. Maybe, because he was different from the other wealthy looking men. His suit was visibly well worn but nevertheless immaculately clean and spotless, and perfectly ironed. His posture was that of pride, and his steps were wide and firm. In his hand, he held a cane with an ivory handle, swinging it back and forth as he walked. I have not seen this gentleman before. The stranger had reached almost the middle of the street walking against the wind, but the strength of the wind was increasing, making walking even more difficult. With one swift and strong blow, the wind suddenly ripped the hat off the gentleman's head. But this stranger was unfazed. He turned his head slowly and gracefully and watched his hat bobbing on the pavement, being taken by the wind further and further away

I saw this gentleman a few more times after this episode. Each time he was dressed to the nines, but now without a hat. He walked proud giving the world an opportunity to see his greying hair combed back in a perfect hairstyle. What is most surprising, since then I started to see more and more gentlemen with uncovered heads. The conclusion to this story is simple – to change the people around you start changing yourself and the rest will follow.

Tale Nineteen

The future and the now

"Do you ever think about the future?" – I asked the Kensington Fairy.

"No," - she said without hesitation. - "It is not necessary to think about the future. The future just needs to be made. And it should be made right now. A gardener plants flower seeds today, but the flowers don't grow until later in the future. He made that future to happen while he was in the now. Similarly, everyone must begin making their future in advance, now. To build a happy future people must start acting upon it now. Imagine that the florist didn't have those flower seeds in time to sell to the gardener. The gardener then couldn't plant those seeds. The flowers that are so pleasant to everyone looking at them would have not grown. Instead, there would be an empty black patch on the ground. What you see today on that flower bed had been made way back in the past."

"I absolutely agree with you," – I had to admit, regretfully. - "Unfortunately, I can only think about the future but cannot do anything about it."

"You are an exception," – agreed the Fairy. - "There is a good reason why you can't do anything. You are a stone lion, you cannot even move. But I tell you what - many people live their lives as if they were stone lions."

Tale Twenty

The rise and fall, the fall and rise

Imagine this situation – a man walks along the street then suddenly stumbles and falls down. What will he do? Naturally, he will get up, shake the street dust off his clothes, straighten up and continue on his way. It is quite predictable. No one will stay down on the ground after the fall if they can get up.

It is quite different what people do with their lives. Sometimes they don't act in a logical manner at all.

Some people are very advanced in their lives, they have progressed and achieved a lot, they have reached high success. But being successful doesn't make people invincible, everyone can fall down. The higher they reach the more dramatic is their fall. Some are able to shake off the 'dust' of failure, straighten up and keep going forward. Others – not so much so. They get up and shake off the dust all right, but the fall makes them stop on their way – they will go neither forward nor back. And there are also those who stay down after their fall... Maybe they cannot get up? Maybe they cannot be bothered. Who knows?

Majority people will walk around navigating the street, navigating the life pretending they see nothing that is not relevant to them, or that nothing is wrong. They become mentally blind. They pretend, or genuinely believe, it's nothing to do with them and the person who had fallen is OK staying down. There are others who look at the fallen ones with interest, some even utter the words of sympathy, but they continue on their own merry way. Some of those who stop may not even pretend to be nice, they would say something offensive, insulting, or even kick the fallen person. Only a small percentage of people will stop and help them up.

Getting up, rising up after a great fall is not easy; otherwise everyone would have done that. But helping someone up is not easy either. The more people pass the fallen ones without helping them, the greater is the chance that when they fall nobody will lend them a helping hand.

And the law of averages proves it's not the matter of 'if' but the matter of 'when'.

Tale Twenty One

Living in a rush

"Ah, these people! They never have enough time for anything!" – reproached the Kensington Fairy observing the bustling of people on the street.

"Why is that surprising?"- I did not understand straight away what she meant by this. - "They can walk from place to place, it takes time".

"So? I can move from place to place too," – enthused the Fairy. - "They just do not know how to appreciate the value of time."

"Do you know how to?" - I was curious.

"Yes, I do!" –exclaimed the Fairy proudly. - "I learnt how to value the time. I have actually cast a spell on the clock on the tower near our garden, so that one minute in an hour has only forty seconds not the usual sixty".

"What for?" – I was amused.

"When you live a life where a minute consists of 50 or 40 seconds, then 60 seconds will seem to you a very, very long time. So long, that you will not allow yourself the luxury of spending it doing nothing". – The Fairy paused, and then continued. - "I have watched people; they don't notice the difference between forty and sixty seconds. They can do as much in forty as they do in sixty. When people value their time they manage to do everything despite of how busy they are. And those who do not know how to appreciate the time cannot do a single thing even if they have an entire day at their disposal".

After a bit of thinking, I decided not to comment on the Fairy's conclusion, because I, personally, am not in a rush.

Tale Twenty Two

The lottery ticket

Once upon a time, a young man sat on my stone paw and solemnly began to scratch off the silver foil from the instant lottery ticket he purchased. He had an expression on his face as if he couldn't care less about the results. He was staring into the distance, far away, or may be just staring into space. His indifference was deceptive, because a minute later, after he carefully glanced at the ticket now showing the winning numbers, he lifted his head up and looked into the sky. He then softly said: "Thank you, Lord. You did not make me happier by sending these winnings and my dream did not materialise. But you helped to resolve my financial problems and now it will be much easier to pursue my dream. I also plead you not to forget me in your future blessings".

Why do I remember this man? Because, despite his young years, he understood something that not every old or mature man is be able to grasp: even the Lord cannot make a person happy, because the happiness comes from within the man's soul. He understood that money is not an end but a means to an end, having lots of money should not be a dream. Money can only serve to support him towards achieving his dream.

The man was very young and clearly inexperienced because of his young years, but he was wise enough to understand that one should speak to God not only in times of need, but always be grateful in times of prosperity.

Tale Twenty Three

The strength and the power

There is not much traffic on my street. Not vehicles, anyway. There are quite a few pedestrians and skateboarders though. These people are quite skilful, they don't just ride up and down the street but do various tricks, difficult and challenging ones, and sometimes those tricks get quite risky. I have noticed that it doesn't take much to fall down even for the most experienced ones. All they need a small pebble getting in between the wheels of a skateboard, or a chipped piece of pavement, and they stumble or fall down.

Watching them fall made me think – it is not necessary to be strong and big to accomplish something great. The willingness, the determination and the skill are important. It doesn't always take a big misfortune to bring people down. A tiny pebble can make a big impact.

The Kensington Fairy told me there are some massive stones that are sitting on the ground, sedentary. They cannot be moved like the pebbles. People call them mountains. But these huge mountains are made out of stone, and are covered by small stones too. Sometimes, a crack may appear in a big rock, or a small stone may break away, starting a big fall of rocks. Imagine, one small stone can trigger a huge rolling of stones from the mountain, the one that didn't want to stay in its place. This illustrates that it's not the size or the strength is important to get the mountain moving. Small cracks in the mountain or a small piece of the broken stone do not have much power, but they can cause real chaos, depending where that crack is. It's not the power itself but the point where that power was applied that matters.

Tale Twenty Four

The couple

Over the years, I have seen many couples using my pedestal as a place to take a break from walking. Some sat there just to give their feet some rest. Others have spent hours sitting at my feet, hiding behind my stone body from the eyes of other pedestrians. There had been so many couples that I have lost the count, some of their stories have already faded or got completely erased from my memory, now buried under a layer of more recent memories. But one couple was different and the memory of them remains with me, no matter how many years have passed.

The summer sunset was particularly lovely with the beauty that only fragile things can carry, with the beauty that could fall apart any second: like the sculpture in the sand can be washed off the shore by the high tide, like the dance of the colourful autumn leaves blown away by the wind.

I don't think stopping by the back gate of the museum was this couple's original plan; they just got so entranced by a beautiful sunset that they had to stop and admire it. The couple have interrupted their stroll and just stood there enjoying the glorious view and the colours of the sun going down to sleep, all the while the young man was whispering something into the girl's ear. Finally, the sun had gone hiding behind the horizon line (as it always had since the beginning of the world) and the magic had disappeared. The young lady glanced at her wristwatch and hurried up to leave.

This happened long ago when the buses were still going on my street. The couple rushed to the bus stop where the bus just arrived. The girl kissed her boyfriend goodbye and hopped on the last bus.

The young man was visibly annoyed, remaining at the bus stop alone. I expected him to be upset, but no, he was not upset but clearly annoyed. He walked towards me and sat down on my pedestal. After a while he began talking: "No matter how many times I talk to her I seem to never have enough time to say everything. So now I want to tell her the most important thing, something that is more important than anything else. The most important are the words of love. But the trouble is, I still cannot say all the words of love either as there are so many of them and so little time!"

Having said that, the young man turned away and shouted out loud: "I love her! Do you hear me, world? I love her!"

I understood that the boy was annoyed with himself. I have thought about these words for a long time and will remember them forever. The human life is short, so why do people spend so much of invaluable time with small talk? Why is there so much anger and misunderstanding in human relationships? Maybe because people spend too much time on talking nonsense and end up having no time for the most important words?

Tale Twenty Five

The light

During long and cold winter evenings it gets dark early. The night descends upon the world fast and people hurry to get home quickly, to be safe, comfortable and warm in their cosy lounges. This is when the street lights come to life, this is their time. One by one, they come to life. First, the lights are dimmed because there is no need for bright illumination when it's still only dusk. The lamps inside the lampposts shimmer, they twinkle tentatively as if thinking – do I need to go full blast already? As the evening advances, the natural light is gone – now the streetlights need to do some real work, some heavy duty work. Who else? What would happen if they didn't work? How would people find their way home, their way anywhere? Even I, the Stone Lion, feel the darkness surrounding me, and it does get spooky and scary at times. In the dark, you can hear many sounds yet cannot see what makes them. Is that not scary enough for you? It is indeed for me. I cannot move, you see? What if the sound means something dangerous and I cannot even retaliate? OK, even in the bright sunshine I still cannot retaliate as I am permanently positioned in one spot. But at least I can prepare, mentally. The street lights help me do that when there is no daylight, they help me, and they help everyone.

You think this is just electricity? Just the technology? The mechanics? Oh, no. Everything is alive. Even something that seemed to be operated by man. The street lamps are the light warriors. They bravely fight the darkness; they light up the world and defeat the murk. Of course, just one lamppost cannot illuminate an entire street; its light covers only a small patch on the ground and a small space surrounding it.

But, there is no such a lamppost that spreads the darkness around itself, like some people do. If only every person brightened up the space around themselves, the world would forget about the gloom.

Sharp edges

I was born out of two main forces of this world: nature and magic. Nature has created the stone, then a sculptor not known to me had carved my body out of it, and the enchanted Kensington Fairy had breathed life into the sculpture so I became alive. This amalgamation of two very different entities, Nature and Magic, made me a creation of nature and magic. So here I am now – the Stone Lion with a living soul and an infinitely long life, but my stone body is still affected by the environment.

Nature loathes any sharp angles and edges. Nature intends everything to be organic and natural. Initially, the law of harmony and smooth lines prevailed. The sharpness was invented and created by mankind. The jagged edges, the sharply protruding corners and peaks are now favoured by the celebrated contemporary artists. These edges are everywhere – in the architecture, in paintings, in patterns.

This sharpness goes totally against nature. And so Mother Nature uses every opportunity and every tool available to smooth those lines – the water currents and the coastal waves transform the sharp-edged rough rocks fallen off the cliffs into rounded and smooth pebbles.

The nature doesn't like rough and jagged, sharp and piercing. Only people do. They like this sharpness in everything material and immaterial; they create it and bring it into their lives too, through rough behaviour and razorblade words. The abrasiveness in their lives had now become a norm. The word 'edgy' had acquired a new meaning – something to be proud of because you are different. But are you really that different if everyone else is also 'edgy'?

But, if your life appears that way, should you try and smooth it out yourself, or, perhaps, you could allow nature take its course?

Tale Twenty Six

Patience is virtue

There was a time when buses were going past my street. Did I say that before? Yes, I did. And to be honest, I am disappointed that the bus route had changed and no longer includes my street. I used to enjoy watching people gathering at the bus stop, waiting for the bus.

For example, the following situation often took place. A man would walk towards the bus stop with a big stride, obviously in a rush. He would stand there, shifting impatiently from one foot to another, glancing at his watch – and still no bus in sight. The man would exchange annoyed glances and words with the others waiting on the bus stop. People may engage in a conversation about the bus service being so poor that they may as well not have the bus service at all. People would keep looking at the bus timetable intently; as if the more they look the sooner the bus comes. They may ask each other how long they have been waiting, and whether any bus had gone past during that time. As if this would change anything and the bus would come sooner.

I don't think they hope their shared annoyance would change anything but at least it helps to pass the time waiting, and people can feel they are not alone.

This would continue for a few minutes until someone would lose their cool and in frustration would walk away at a speed, almost running. No sooner as this person turns the street corner, the bright red double-decker would arrive.

Such a scene is very common, showing that a little perseverance would have served that man better than his impatience. If you cannot see the task through to completion, is it worth starting it?

Tale Twenty Seven

The tree

When I look at the mighty tree growing nearby, I remember the time when it was just a young branch planted by a gardener. Back then, it was a small tree barely rising above the ground. But despite its tiny size and the harsh weather, the tree was stubborn and kept seeking the sunlight and growing without fear. It wasn't scared of storms or the caterpillars devouring its small green leaves. Every time the storm would bend the young tree and pin it to the ground, the tree had inevitably risen up and proudly straightened up again, spreading its new branches towards the sun. For every green leaf chewed up by the caterpillar the tree had grown a few new leaves.

This tree had survived a lot during its lifetime – the bitter winds and droughts, thunderstorms and lightning, and even the bombing of London during the wars. Its branches remember it all. Its branches are now strong and nothing could break the tree. Once a tiny twig, the tree had learnt to be resilient and is now sturdy and stands proud, giving a shelter in its branches to the many birds.

Strength is not something you are born with. You need to work at it, you need to build it. Strength is not something that is being granted. You need to learn to be strong and that is not easy. Some powerful people are believed to be strong – not always true. Strength and power are not always the same. You can be powerful because it's part of your personality. It doesn't mean you are guaranteed to stay strong and not to crumble in hard times. The tree had been through many of a hard time and it stood strong. I look at this giant now and understand that to become great and strong you need to survive more than a dozen storms.

Tale Twenty Eight

The saxophonist

Some people think of buskers as a nuisance. Pedestrians walk past trying not to notices them, not to make an eye contact with the busker who may smile and then the pedestrian would feel guilty if they don't drop a coin into an open guitar case, or into a hat placed on the floor, or into a used coffee cup. I used to like buskers, but, to my regret, they do not favour my street for their performances. I reckon, this must be due to the fact that there are not enough pedestrians for the buskers to earn decent money. Majority of the museum visitors use the main gate.

When I first saw a busker I didn't know there is such a line of work. Once, when it was already fairly late, a young musician decided to perform on my street. He carried a large weirdly looking shape case. Once he chose the spot to settle on, he took the case off his shoulders, opened it and took out a shiny instrument. Later, the Kensington Fairy explained it was a musical instrument, a saxophone. Having finished all his preparations, the young man began to play and the music started to fill the evening air. It was very beautiful – an empty street and the sounds of music floating in the darkness.

It seemed he was playing not for anyone else but for himself. Maybe, he simply didn't have another place where he could play at this late hour. Maybe, he was on his way somewhere and had a moment of inspiration. I don't know.

But it doesn't matter. The man was making the music and was obviously happy. It is good when a person feels inspired and happy. It is common nowadays for people to hide their emotions from others, to suppress their feelings. I am fearful that sometime soon people might forget the feelings and emotions altogether, they might forbid themselves from feeling anything. They would forget how to be happy in the moment as opposed to the publicly accepted rules.

This is not how I hope to see people; I hope to see them emotional. I want to see people cry when they are upset. I want to hear them laugh when something is funny. Emotions should not be restrained. This life is not a prison for emotions; they should be felt and expressed.

Tale Twenty Nine

The Tales of a Stone Lion

Home is where the heart is

I often witness groups of people having fun. One quiet evening a small group of people decided to sit down on the pedestal and get some rest. They were cheerful, full of joy and laughter, enjoying each other's company, exchanging pleasantries and kind jokes. I enjoyed such evenings too, I could do with having some fun, and happy people are always fun to be around. However, no matter how well they got on together, and how nice the night was under the clear starry sky, they still all went home their separate ways.

I did not fully understand why these people had to part if they were so happy together. But one time, the Kensington Fairy explained to me the reason for this. No matter how good the time they had together, how quiet and pleasant was the evening in an empty street, or how interesting the conversation was, no matter how extraordinary the beauty of such gatherings was – they all went *home*. The greatest joy people feel is when they return home. Home – it is safe and comfortable, it is warm and light there. There are other people who they love waiting for them at home. There is more laughter and kindness and happiness to be felt at home.

I have heard the saying *'home is where the heart is'*. I now understand the meaning. If you return home and don't feel happy and peaceful, then you must have come to the wrong house where your heart does not belong.

Tale Thirty

The music of nature

I have quite a lot of free time. Indeed, as I am unable to move, to leave my permanent abode which is a pedestal at the museum's back gates, I tend to study the world around me using only two senses available to me – my sight and my hearing. Over many years, I have learned to listen very carefully and attentively to every little sound. I have learned to distinguish between the hubbub of a big city, between the urban sounds and the other sounds that interest me. But most of all I like to listen to the music of nature.

Everything has its own music. The quiet rustle of drizzling rain falling from the sky, this too, is the music of nature. The sounds of thunderstorms are also the nature's music: the rumblings of thunder, the roaring wind and then the heavy raindrops hitting the ground – now, this is not just a piece of music, but the whole orchestra with different instruments each playing their own part. There is music of the day, and music of the night. The silence of the night is occasionally broken by the sound of a bird flapping its wings in the darkness, the crickets chirping in the overgrown lawns, the whooshing and rustling sounds of the wind blowing dry leaves over the paved road. All this is accompanied by the stars winking to one another and to the people below – this, in my opinion, is the most beautiful musical show in the world.

The Kensington Fairy said that when she and her fairy sisters get lonely or sad, they ask the flowers to sing their wonderful and colourful songs. Unfortunately, people can't hear the flowers, neither can I. But it doesn't mean the flowers cannot sing. It simply means that during the day it is too noisy for anyone but the fairies to hear the flowers' songs, and at night the flowers are sleeping. People cannot see the colours of a song, but the fairies can. The nature is full of music and you can hear it all if you stop running for just one minute and open your heart and mind to receive the beauty.

Pattern of a human life

I said this some time ago, and I like repeating it now and again, because this concept seems very important. The destiny, the pattern of a human life is similar to those of a spider web. The threads and knots of a web are weightless and graceful; each line is unique and cannot be repeated or duplicated, ever. Some threads of this beautiful yarn created by a spider can be found hanging like a hammock between the branches of a tree, there are translucent and delicate lace of a web wrapped around lampposts and window frames.

Similarly, each person has his own destiny and his own place in the world. Some are attached, others are detached.

But the spider webs are not permanently fixed to any place where the spider had created them. When a strong wind blows the parts of a lace off, the small detached net begins its way through the air and the ideal lace pattern no longer exists. It should not be forgotten that it is impossible to create a perfect pattern of a human life either.

Tale Thirty One

The pedestrians

There are thousands of different people walking up and down my street, some faces look familiar. Some of them know each other. Some people know each other by sight.

Others are complete strangers. Some people only ever walk my street once, others might walk in one direction first and then I see them coming back from wherever they have been. I am interested in every person whom I see on my street, whether they do look familiar or not. Because every person is unique, every person is an individual with their own life story, with their own destiny. Every person has their own personal feelings and emotions. Some people have their stories written all over their faces, others are hiding it.

Each person is connected to all the others by the invisible thread of a human life. I do not know who all these strangers are – some might be selfish, others could be philanthropists, they might be successful businessmen or skilful workers, intelligent politicians or great musicians, philosophers or mathematicians. It does not make any difference. I am equally interested in them all. To me, they all are fragile living creatures with their own unspoken secrets.

I think it is absolutely irrelevant who has succeeded in life and who has not. I neither care nor differentiate between someone who looks a millionaire and another who is a beggar. How is this important? Who can decide what success is, anyway? Who can say that the millionaire is rich and the beggar is poor? What is the measure of wealth – just the money? What about the wealth of feelings, the wealth of experience. I cannot label people as successful or unsuccessful when I don't even know their stories. Each person is a miracle and a mystery. I would also emphasise – a fragile and unique miracle. Therefore, all should be treated as such.

Tale Thirty Two

A fox

In the garden of one of the residential houses located nearby the museum once lived a young fox.

The residents of the house didn't mind at all. The fox did not bother them; it did not do any harm. While living in a close proximity with people the fox had become a somewhat domesticated animal. In fact, it was so tame that the house owners' little daughter made friends with the little fox and could safely play with its fluffy red tail as if it were a soft toy!

However, although the girl's parents didn't mind the presence of the fox they were objecting very much to this friendship. To put an end to his daughter's friendship with the fox, the father got a big and vicious dog to scare the fox out of the garden. The fox was small and friendly and loved the little girl, but the dog was too big and too scary for the fox. The fox had left the garden and never came back.

The dog, on the other hand wasn't afraid of anything or anyone. It grew to disrespect its own master and became unruly. It was intimidating not only the fox but also the little girl and her parents. The girl's father was not a weak man but he no longer felt like coming out into the garden, he didn't want to meet his own dog. It was now the dog who ruled in the garden. The little girl was very scared of the dog's growling and constant barking at everyone coming close to the garden. Because nobody had trained the dog to be a guard dog, it became a bully snarling at everything and everyone coming near the garden fence. It was barking even at the birds flying over the yard! The little fox was peaceful; it got frightened of the dog and went elsewhere.

The fox had found another garden where it was welcomed, but it missed the friendship of the little girl, and the girl was also inconsolable over her one and only friend who was now lost forever. If only her father didn't assume that he knows better what she really needs.

Tale Thirty Three

Nature changes constantly

I like the early autumn days when the crowns of the trees on my street are covered by multi-coloured leaves. There are yellow and red leaves, some are rusty-coloured, and other trees retain their green canopies the whole year.

Each leaf of the same tree has a different pattern and changes its colour differently. There are a different number of leaves and branches that each tree has – some branches get broken and the leaves fall off, new branches and new leaves grow before the next autumn begins. Different leaves change their colours on the same tree every year. You'd think the difference would stop here? No. Different trees change their colours at different times, and the tree that was mostly red last autumn may be half-green and half-yellow this year. And this is so fascinating! The colour pattern on my street is never the same the following autumn. Just imagine that all these years since I have been guarding the museum nature had never repeated its pattern, not once!

This is because Nature is not static – it constantly changes. Everything is subject to change, everything is moving, and there is never a repetition of the same pattern in nature. Even the landscape doesn't stay still – the ocean's waters can flood the land, but the sea shores change shape too.

During my long life, many times have I seen the small drops of rain on the pavement joining the bigger drops, forming a puddle and eventually flooding the street. This can easily prove one simple postulate that even a small effort is worth a lot, because put together small efforts can make a significant change.

Tale Thirty Four

The small details

    I have been watching people's behaviour for a long time, and have a strong belief that the inner core of a human, his essence, can be seen through his actions, through the small details of his actions. Not through the great events that are on everyone's mind, but through the little things which many people don't pay much attention to, or put any value on. Through the body language, or by how they treat others, and by how they react to the people that have upset them. The real person can be seen through the small acts they do or they don't, by the words they say or don't say, by the way they look at others and at themselves.

These little actions seem insignificant and not easily noticed in a crowd. For example, if a well-dressed man is rude to an old little lady who accidentally trod on his shiny polished shoe. Or someone is smoking in public waving their hand with a cigarette in it without giving any consideration to the others, accidentally burning a hole in the dress of a girl who happened to walk past. You may not notice any of this when too many people are around, but it will stand out if you watch carefully. You may notice the little old lady apologising because her foot happened to be in that man's way. The young girl may say 'sorry' to the smoker because she didn't move away from the burning cigarette. You see all this and decide for yourselves, who is doing a good deed there and who is not, who pays attention to details and who doesn't.

People often try to present themselves better than they really are. Many think of themselves higher than they deserve. That is the conclusion I made. Why do they think that way? I do not understand, because by having a false heightened opinion of themselves people won't deceive others.

Tale Thirty Five

Any weather is fine weather

One very hot summer, a fresh green grass blade sprouted through the cracks between the stones, right beside me. It was a very bold and brave sprig because it was not afraid to grow alone in the middle of the stone pavement.

I liked the little green sprig very much; it was talkative and lively so we became good friends. It was also very inquisitive and asked many questions, about anything – what kind of outfits people wore a hundred years ago, what magical creatures I have met in my lifetime. The green sprig was young and very curious. The grass doesn't live a long life, not like people. But I think as people grow older their natural curiosity imperceptibly gives way to indifference.

My little young friend was very happy with having an extended period of sunny days and did not understand how I could possibly like the rain. But, with time, because of the hot sun and the lack of rain, my friend started to feel unwell and because the weather stayed sunny for a long time, without a rain the green sprig became dehydrated and very ill. Fortunately, these sunny days don't last forever and after a long period of dry weather the heavy shower watered the ground and the grass blade finally got its long awaited drink of water. My friend, even though very young, had now realised – it cannot and it must not be fine weather all the time. There must be rain and thunderstorms, otherwise permanent sun will burn everything to the ground, so the rainy days are also fine days.

Tale Thirty Six

The clown's truth

One night I was approached by a very drunken person dressed as a clown. He was quite unsteady on his feet. He put his hand on my body and leaned against me, almost falling down. He then fished out an almost empty bottle of some liquid from the depth of his robe, took a sip, and burst into tears.

He wept quietly with his tears running down his face. He was smearing his heavy makeup over his face with his hands and getting it onto the frills of his white blouse's sleeves.

"Tired", - he said, nodding to himself, or maybe to me. - "You know, buddy, I am so tired to go out to that god awful stage and talk nonsense to amuse the crowd. I've had enough!"

Having said this, he burst into tears again. When, after a few minutes he calmed down he continued: "Do you think I talk nonsense to them? You think I make jokes? Huh, if only! I actually tell them the truth and they, in their stupidity or blindness, think I'm cracking jokes, and they laugh. I tell them the real stories about people I have witnessed. I tell them the real stories from my own life. I tell them the stories that could have, and probably have, happened to so many of them. But they don't even realize they laugh at each other and themselves, not at me."

After resting for some time at the feet of my pedestal, the clown shock his head as in disbelief, got up and walked away wobbling on his feet from side to side, leaving me alone with my thoughts about how people are strange creatures – they believe in the absurd and lies told by those in the high positions, yet they don't believe the truth when it's told by a clown.

Tale Thirty Seven

The talking trees

During dark autumn nights the moist and cold air of London chills even my stone body. The branches of a giant tree growing nearby make these exceptionally sad creaking sounds when they are moving in the wind. The sound is like that of someone crying. Only a few people know that these are not just the creaks of the dry branches but, indeed, are the sad sobs of the old tree being tormented by the nightmares from its past.

The trees can talk. They talk to me. If you learn to listen you will hear them too. One hot summer day the tree told me about its dreams, about the nightmares caused by the memories of the bombing of London. People were suffering and nobody paid attention to the trees which were also suffering. They were being chopped off, torn into shreds, and used as fuel for fires going up in flames. I remember seeing this happening to the trees during the war; I have heard their pain and cries. I have seen young trees dying as well as hundred year's old oaks. Since then, as soon as I hear the sad creaking of the branches of a sleeping tree, I immediately call for help. I call for the fairies. My little friend the Kensington Fairy has this gift to quickly push all the nightmares away and let the tree sleep in peace. Remember the flower songs that the fairies listen to when they are frightened? The Fairy and her little sisters sing the songs they heard from the flowers to the trees, the same songs that calm the fairies calm the trees too.

The trees can talk of course; they ask for help and get the magical help of the fairies to cure their nightmares. People don't need fairies to rid of their nightmares. A loving person being close, their caring and comforting words help. Just being near the person who loves you or the person your love can help. Because people are also magicians, they must not forget it.

Tale Thirty Eight

An angry world

My life is quite extraordinary. Having to remain on the same spot for centuries I have an opportunity to watch people, generation after generation. Indeed, I cannot observe the same person's whole life but only when they happen to be in front of my eyes and within my hearing range, but I have concluded that mankind becomes much angrier and more cynical as the times go by.

I have shared my observations with the Kensington Fairy and she, in turn, shared her own thoughts on this fact – this is because there are more and more people, but fewer trees. The population grows fast, people cut down the forest to clear the space for their own needs, to build more houses, to use the timber. People do not seem to realise that trees not only produce oxygen but also absorb all the gloom and misery, the pessimism and anger. The trees collect all negative emotions from people and ground them. Although, even if people knew that, it is unlikely the situation would have changed. The world is becoming more and more populated and the collective negative emotions are becoming thicker and more prominent.

The forests, on the contrary, are fewer, and there are not enough trees around the densely populated areas to disperse all the negativity. This inevitably leads to the imbalance of the good and bad, and the human world is becoming a place full of anger and indifference.

If I could talk to people, I would ask them not to cut down trees, but rather to plant new ones. Then you would look around and see that the world had become greener and kinder.

Tale Thirty Nine

The escape

My street. What is actually my street? It is only a short stretch of the road, the space sandwiched between the buildings. When the wind is blowing across the river, or in the fields, it has plenty of space for free flow, to speed up. The wind grows stronger and faster, and then it suddenly finds itself trapped in an almost enclosed space, between the buildings standing on both sides of my street. The wind is now strong, it struggles to flow. What is the wind to do? It cannot just stop and hang in the air; so to speak, it has to continue forward whichever way 'forward' means. After all, if the wind stops, it will cease to be the wind and will turn into something else. So the wind keeps moving forward, backwards, it is trapped between these stone walls. It bounces off the walls, howling, whistling, trying to rush forward, to escape...

I mentioned this to the Kensington Fairy, musing – what would happen to people in such a situation? What if people were trapped between something as the wind often does?

She thought for a while then said: "People feel trapped too. Imagine a child growing up with parents who have a very strong authority. The child will grow with conflict between what he or she wants to be, and what the parents want them to be. The relationship will become stormy, and, eventually, the child will feel trapped and won't be able to contain his or her own desires any longer and will have to escape, just like the wind."

Tale Forty

The safe haven

My friend Black Raven, who visits me occasionally, says: "There is nothing more pleasant than seeing a beacon of light atop a lighthouse pointing you to the safe harbour during the dark stormy night, it is a pure haven."

Each one of us has our own private haven. For the fairies this safe haven is a flower bud of any big colourful flower growing in Kensington Gardens. The gentle and fragile flower petals serve as the walls of protection for these little magical creatures, hiding them from all the troubles of the outside world. For the Black Raven, the grim stones and walls of the Tower of London epitomises safe haven. For some, it is a tree house built by their fathers. For others, it is a lounge in their home filled with the voices of the loved ones. For some people, safe haven is a memory of the good times they had. The options are vast, but every safe haven has that beacon of light that makes it visible and welcoming. Only the lighthouse is capable of breathing life into the dark harbour, and it can take you away from the safety by switching off the beacon. Find that light in your safe haven.

It should be remembered that only the lighthouse is able to breathe life into the harbour, and the lighthouse master is the one switching it on or off. You are the lighthouse master.

Tale Forty One

One step back

Since I cannot move, it is not surprising that so many events pass me by, because they happen in other parts of London. I know London is a lot bigger than just the space around me but I cannot see those parts. My world is small, it consists only of one street, but my friends do travel around and tell me the city is actually much, much bigger than what is visible to me. I, therefore, rely on my friends to tell me what they have seen in those other parts of the city. Fortunately, my friends tell me some of the stories that I have missed. Here is one such a story, as told by the Black Raven.

Once, he saw a young woman had climbed to the top of the Tower Bridge railing. She looked as if she was intending to throw herself down, off the bridge, but she hesitated. She stood there gripping tightly to the cold metal railing while the crowd was gathering on the ground below. People's faces showed different expressions, and there was a lot of murmur – some were expecting her to jump down, others were horrified. This was a very long time ago, when women wore long skirts and hats, before the motorcars took over the streets and lot of people were walking.

One young man was brave enough to climb up the railing. Once he reached the girl he stood there holding tight and talked. Both were very high up and people could not hear what they were saying. My friend Black Raven didn't hear their conversation either. Somebody must have called the police, but when the rescuers arrived the girl refused to talk to anyone other than this guy. He finally persuaded her not to go forward but to take a step back, and to go down safely. They both climbed down with the guy helping that girl to safety.

People were commending the young man, calling him a hero but he kept praising the girl for not having jumped off the bridge. He didn't explain the detail but obviously she must have told him something, if he considered it very brave for the girl to continue living this life. This story told me that sometimes one step back is worth more than a hundred steps forward.

Tale Forty Two

The past and the future

Many years ago, a road accident happened on my street and a young lady was injured. Fortunately, at that time the cars were not as fast as they are now so the lady had survived. It was a great joy for me to know that she was alive as I value human life highly.

After a while, I noticed that the girl injured in that accident started visiting me every evening. She did nothing else but sat at the foot of my pedestal and stared into the space. I could not follow the direction of her eyes, so I assume she looked at the street, perhaps at the spot where the accident took place. But I could sense that she was very upset by something. Any pedestrian could simply assume that she was thoughtful or waiting for someone, sitting here. I knew better as I witnessed the accident. This girl was very sad indeed.

She kept coming every day for over a year and, despite being grateful for any visitor, any company, I didn't like her visits. I understood, she didn't just come to sit there, to rest, to think of something. She came to re-live her experience. She was stuck in that sad and painful past, recollecting the sequence of events and feelings in her head day after day, thus putting off living her life – now, and in the future.

I saw this young lady incapable to shift the burden of the past from her soul, to let it rest, to accept and move on. I couldn't help her either; I don't have any magic powers. So I called upon my precious friend, the Kensington Fairy. The fairy is small and her powers are limited but it was enough to pull the girl out of the grip of her past. After that, I have seen the girl a few more times. I could see the sadness in her eyes, but it was the sadness of past experience, not the sadness for the future. I understood that now the lady would be able to continue living, to move forward.

The Kensington Fairy said: "A person who lives in the past has no future. But it can be also said, anyone without a past had not lived".

Tale Forty Three

The flowers

Flowers are beautiful; they are like the stars descended from heavens. I love when the gentlemen give their ladies flowers in front of my pedestal, or anywhere on my street. I reckon, people can learn a lot from those thin stems and weightless petals – persistence and determination, courage and the zest for life.

Think of one flower, just one single flower – how much joy can it bring to a person. I have seen sour looking faces light up with a smile, tears of sadness turning into tears of joy or pleasure, simply because of a single flower. It doesn't matter whether the flower was an exquisite rose, a luxurious peony, an elegant gladiola or a beautiful but understated tulip. It doesn't matter if it's only a single flower or a bouquet. I have seen ladies turning from sad to happy with a single daffodil.

Every spring I watch the flight of tiny flower seeds and pollen anxiously, worrying about each seed that could not fly over the street to land on the grass, settling on the paved stones instead. I want every speck of pollen to land on the fertile grounds so there are more flowers around. Those simple daffodils that grow everywhere, they don't need looking after; they just grow because the pollen has landed where the flower could grow. Not just the view, but the life is so much better when there are lots of flowerbeds around in the city. The colourful buds break up the grey scenery of the buildings.

The Kensington Fairy says that flowers indeed are the stars descended from heaven, because both the stars and the flowers have been bringing people happiness and joy for centuries, and they continue this relentless work of beauty.

Tale Forty Four

Fighting the fear

I really like small children playing around me. I like it when they bravely climb onto my pedestal and then onto my back. Sometimes the adults do too, but this happens very rarely, and then only the young adults would do anything like that in the public. Any mature person would look at them and shake their head disapprovingly. I don't know whether they are afraid of climbing, or are afraid to lose their dignity in front of others. Maybe, both. Adults very rarely put themselves at any risk.

Once, a little girl wanted to climb up onto my back and asked a boy who just slid down from there: "Was that scary? Were you afraid?"

The boy thought his answer over for a moment. He might have wanted to brag and show some bravado but said the truth nonetheless: "Yes, it's scary and I was afraid."

"But you still climbed up there?"- asked the girl.

"Yes, I did" - answered the boy. - "I'm scared all the same, but I imagine that my mum and dad are already up there stretching their arms out to help me climb. I know they will keep me safe so the fear goes away."

There are many people in the world and there are many of their fears: the fear of darkness, of heights, of spiders and more. Some people run away from their fears, others are learning to accept their fears and live with them, and then there are those who conquer their fears. Those who fight, have a chance to overcome their fears. Just like that little boy did. But others are defeated by their fears. Fighting against your fear is simple, yet it is so hard. Believing in yourself, trusting yourself is always difficult because people don't really know their real strength; they don't know what they are capable of. But I have seen many critical situations when seemingly ordinary people acted courageously. Who else can believe in you if you don't believe in yourself? It only takes one flip of your mind to go from fearful to fearless.

Tale Forty Five

The snowflake dance

White snowflakes slowly swirled before my face, so beautiful and so delicate. The first ones were already set on the pavement beneath my paws as a thin sheath of snow, and their fragile white sisters continued to descend from the sky to join them. I sat on my pedestal staring at the snowflake dance and thought – they are so small but they are not weak if they managed to make this long trip down from the clouds. The snowflakes were not afraid of this long fall which appeared as an elegant dance lasting only a few minutes for each white dancer.

I am big and made out of stone, nobody could even think of calling me small or weak – yet, I could not do anything like this. The Kensington Fairy said that there are places in this world, which I have not seen, where the inhabitants have to move the snow with the shovels, sometimes with the snow ploughs. It makes people's lives difficult, and they get frustrated with the snow.

I wonder if people even think about the long path each snowflake has taken to get to the ground. Do they try to count, or estimate, how many snowflakes it takes to create a snowdrift? I don't think many people do. Snowflakes seem weightless; they float in the air without any effort – that is what people think. Often, it doesn't even occur to a human mind that it takes an enormous effort for each snowflake to descend down before it can land on the man's hat, on his shoulder, on my head or near my paws on the pavement. Such is human nature that people judge everything based on the first impression! Yet, that first impression is rarely true, for the simple reason that the result we see never shows how much work had been put into it; we never really know the full path of how things arrive to where they are.

Tale Forty Six

The fire

One bright and hot summer two friends have sat on my pedestal and chatted. I didn't hear the whole conversation but caught the tail end of it. One young man was telling another about the fire at the hotel where he worked.

"... so they took us all outside and had us standing there for 3 hours, until the fire was extinguished, and still carried out the checks throughout the entire building after they checked we have all evacuated".

"So what happened in the end?" – asked his friend with an interest.

"Well, it turned out a couple of hotel rooms apparently have burned out completely and they had to close the whole floor because of that. I don't really know the rest".

"Did they tell you how the fire started?" – The friend was curious.

"Apparently, one of the guests took up smoking in a non-smoking room. Worse still, allegedly, he was flicking the ash from his cigarette on to the bed! *Very intelligent*!"

The two friends sat silent for a while then the first guy continued:

"You know, so many times I stood outside of that hotel and thought how much I hate it, I even wished it to burn to ashes. In the heat of a moment, that is, of course. But when the fire started and my wishes almost came true, I panicked. I suddenly realised that I had nowhere else to go, I mean, for work. So if this hotel did burn down, what would I do? What happened yesterday completely changed my outlook on my work".

Then the friend got up and left. It was midday and the lunchtime must have finished. I was left alone with the tourists rushing by, but reminiscing this conversation I was thinking that some people, indeed, don't know how to appreciate what they have until they lose, or almost lose it.

Tale Forty Seven

The angel's song

One warm summer day an angel descended from heaven. I won't be describing him as I don't want to reduce his appearance to the description in human words.

This angel told me he had a task to complete here on Earth, but then he saw me and felt like chatting to me first. I guess, sometimes the angels want to talk to the stone lions. Our conversation lasted many hours, the angel showed no signs of being in a rush and I certainly was in no hurry to be anywhere else. As the time went by and our discussion continued, it was already the evening, then a short summer night was upon us with the sky full of stars.

Raising his head to the sky the angel said:

"The stars are very curious. Every night they come out into the sky to watch people. That is why the night sky full of stars. Even when people can't see the stars because of the clouds, the stars can still see them."

"Why do the stars want to know all about people? Out of curiosity?" – I asked, intrigued.

"Yes, indeed" – confirmed the angel.

"Who are the stars, really? Tell me?" – I was very interested.

"If I was to tell you about the stars, I would have to tell their whole story right from the beginning. I do not have the time for that" – apologised the angel, - "but I will sing for you the song of human dreams, instead".

Having said that, the angel began to sing. This was the most divine melody I have ever heard, but, to my great regret, he did not sing for a long time. The song is still replaying in my head, and not a single note from it had subsided. The song was short, but I now know why people go to sleep – they do it to hear the angels singing in their dreams.

Tale Forty Eight

People on my street

"Many people live nowadays using the same principles as their ancient ancestors. They take things as a given without any question, without trying to change what they don't like", - said the Kensington Fairy. - "They wake up with the alarm clock ringing and curse it every morning. They get up, get ready and go out. They walk the street they don't like, they travel to work they hate. And the worst thing is, they are so used to it became the new norm, like the daily sunrise or a sunset. People just cannot imagine things being different, they don't want any change."

"What do you make of this?" – asked the fairy.

"I don't know, really", - I said apologetically. - "I only see people when they get to my street, and even then I see them only for a few moments while they walk past. I am lucky if I see them for a little longer if they stop nearby".

"I can't believe you haven't noticed", - said the Kensington Fairy, clearly not impressed with my response.

After hearing that tone of voice from the fairy I thought long and hard. Did I really pay attention? Did people become different? Have I missed any changes in people that I see regularly? I have noticed, during the last decade, the workmen rushing to work in the factories or on the building sites, have almost completely disappeared from my street. They were humble people, unpretentious, and usually in a good humour. These guys are now replaced by well-dressed and always rushing somewhere businessmen carrying leather folders in their hands. These men almost always look harassed or in a bad temper. With this change of pedestrian types, the atmosphere on my street had changed too.

I had to agree and disagree with the Kensington Fairy. The changes have happened; a big change is inevitable with the progress of time. But the small changes are not that evident. Once a workman – always a workman. Once a businessman – always a businessman. People like putting a label on themselves; they want a routine they are familiar with. It's so easy to introduce something different or new to this routine, even if only changing the route to their work – but most are afraid of doing even that little.

Tale Forty Nine

The black snow

During my long life I have seen many bad and even horrific, shocking actions done by people. Much of these actions were done unconsciously through being indifferent, but there were also plenty of terrible actions that were committed knowingly and maliciously. Although, to me it seems that unintentional or deliberate harm is still evil, all the same.

I have seen London being covered by a deep snow. First, the snow keeps falling and it seems there is not much of it, not just yet. Then, as if suddenly, everything turns white and the set snow is deep, the whole street is hidden underneath the cold white blanket. The earth is snowed under.

That is what happens to people when they do something wrong. They get 'snowed under'. People may make a genuine mistake or misjudgement, something very insignificant. They find a reason or excuse for it, a reasonable explanation. Then they allow more faults to happen, then a little more, and some more… After a while, seeing they could get away with it, they start acting with intent, and before they know they are full of evil.

Just like the snow that covers my street, this evil now covers up the person's soul. Except, while the blanket of snow on my street is clean and white, the evil blanket covering the mean person's soul is black and dirty.

Tale Fifty

The rain and the rainbow

I love the rain, a torrential downpour. I like when the water cuts through the air like a jet in front of my eyes. I like it when the water drops fall down onto my back and then keep running down along the sides of my body, down to the plinth, onto the ground, forming a small puddle that keeps getting bigger as the rain continues. During these moments, the world disappears. The birds don't fly in the rain; they find cover and wait. People do the same; they don't like getting wet and hide underneath the shops' canopies or duck into the arches of the nearby buildings. They wait. Everybody waits for the rain to stop. The life fades giving way to the rain that will clean the pavements, the buildings. It gives way to the rain that will selflessly water the trees and the bushes, clean the leaves from the dust of the city, clear the air...

I love the sun too. Not the scorching heat of July but the soft spring sun bringing light to the world, marking the beginning of life, warming hearts and souls of those who had them frozen during dark and long winter days.

I will never forget the day when I first saw the rainbow. It was a fine spring day, one of those days when the rain seems never-ending, when it looks like it's about to stop, slowing down, and then it suddenly attacks the ground with the new force and more water. The rain eventually stopped and the clouds have parted letting the sun rays through the gaps. In an instant, the colourful semicircle appeared in the sky looking like a dome. I later found this multicolour ribbon was called rainbow and it only appears in the sky after the heavy rain. The rainbow was magnificent; the colours were bright yet translucent. It was undoubtedly very beautiful.

The sun had disappeared behind the clouds again and the rainbow was gone in just a few minutes. I realised that when two powerful forces such as the sun and the rain come together, it's not necessary ending in a catastrophe but a fragile beauty might be born.

Tale Fifty One

The butterflies

Butterflies. There are not as many of them on my street as there are in Kensington Gardens where fairies enjoy listening to the songs of flowers, and where they go to sleep in the soft middles of the flower buds covering up with the petals as if it were blankets.... There are a few butterflies that still fly over my street, and I remember one such a lovely visit in particular.

It was a bright sunny summer day and a very beautiful butterfly with exquisite pattern on her wings had landed on my front paw. She sat there with her delicate quivering wings soaking up the sunrays, bathing in the warmth. Suddenly, as it often happens in London, in the space of a few seconds it was raining. The butterfly's wings are so thin and fragile they soaked in the rain immediately and became wet and heavy, she couldn't fly off my paw and find a shelter to dry her wings. Soon it became windy too, so the butterfly just sat there before me desperately grasping to my paw narrowly escaping being blown off my plinth and into the puddle.

I felt so sorry for the small defenceless butterfly yet I could not help her. She was holding on for dear life with all her might when a strong gust of wind threw a sheet of paper towards my plinth. The paper was already thoroughly soaked and it stuck to my front paw, but it didn't lay flat forming an angle between my body and my foot. This cover wasn't much of a shelter but it did provide enough protection to the butterfly and saved her from being blown off onto the pavement.

After the rain had finished the sun came out again and it was just as warm as before, but it took a long time for the butterfly to dry her wet wings. She sat on my paw for another hour till she was finally able to fly off. It is indeed amazing how a wet sheet from a notebook can save someone's life.

Tale Fifty Two

The door handle

Among many conversations taking place between different people on the steps of my pedestal, I remember this one the most, between an elderly man in an expensive grey coat and his companion, a young man who listened to the old guy with great attention.

"Life is like a corridor with many doors on both sides of it. Sometimes, to open one door you have to close another door. Sometimes, life itself does this for you, opens and closes the doors. But more often than not you have to do it yourself, regardless how scary it may be. People should remember that there isn't a corridor where all the doors are locked and there's is no light no life behind all the doors. All doors cannot be all closed at the same time; at least one door will be unlocked. It is not always possible to find that door easily, on the first attempt. You need to look carefully to see the light seeping through the gap between the door and the door frame, through the keyhole. You need to look for reflection of that light on the floor by your feet. You need to find that door.

Sometimes, you need remarkable strength and even greater courage to pull the door handle. You need to have enough willpower as you might have to try a few different doors until you find the one that is unlocked, unlocked for you. But when you find your door, turn the handle. If you don't open any new doors you will still continue wandering between the same walls of the corridor while several rooms full of light have always been unlocked".

The pair left. The elderly gentleman nodded his head before leaving; he was saying goodbye to me. They were gone, but I was still hearing the voice of Wind of the North – that is how the younger companion addressed the grey haired man – continued to resound in my head, in the whistling of the wind blowing between the buildings on my street: "There are no such doors that won't open to those worthy to see the light behind the door. To open the door you need to simply turn the handle."

Author tales inspired by the tales told by the Stone Lion

***

Don't run, you've got time. The faster you run the faster the time flies away. Slow down, catch your breath, feel the life beating inside your body. You are alive! Feel your life; don't let your everyday routine bury your life energy under the road's dust.

Never forget that you are a star, and you should be shining. It does not matter if you do not have grateful spectators. Stars are shining for themselves not for the spectators. And you are a star! So allow yourself to feel your inner life energy and start shining, not for anybody, but for yourself.

***

The time does not disappear without a trace but settles as a thin film of dust on the surface of the road. It becomes the cracks in the stone buildings and the gaps and cavities in the fortification walls of a castle.

Come near, approach the walls of the ancient palace, take your gloves off and touch the stone with your bare hands. Feel the cold surface of the rock that was roughened and crumbled by time and bad weather. Ask the stone – how many winters and summers had it seen? How many autumns and springs have come and gone? Touch the tree growing in the yard; sense the warmth of its bark with your fingertips. Feel the strength hidden behind the surface, inside the tree. Its core has not given up to the weather; it has not given in to the people.

Imagine yourself being a guest in this world. A guest who had arrived much later than these magnificent giants, and who will leave into the sunset of life much earlier. Feel the touch of all other people who were there before you, who have built the walls and grown the trees that stood in the same place for centuries. Look at your own life with fresh eyes and consider all the milestones you had so far, join the dots and review them – maybe they are not the full stops at all, but only commas?

***

There are days in every person's life when they feel despair. When it seems that everything in life is going down. The worst thing in such situations is that you somehow refuse to see the things are not that bad, really, and you don't understand that everything is only in your mind. In fact, what may seem superficially bad is often not bad at all. But your thoughts are different from your feelings. In your mind, you realise it's not a total disaster, but your feelings tell you that your life is ruined. You begin to see everything as bad, or see bad in everything. You feel empty and abandoned by everyone. You start to wallow in self-pity, you see no solution and the world is now against you.

The bad news – if you continue down this road the misery and bad luck will continue coming into your life. The good news – you have survived such days in the past, haven't you? So you will survive them now, too. Just let them be and go. Tomorrow is a new day, who knows it may bring something good? Accept both.

***

How many times in your life have you started a journey to nowhere? Leaving your home not knowing where are you going to? I usually do this once or twice every month. I just put my clothes on and go out.

When you travel you should remember that life is not just a journey from where you are now to where you want to be. There is often at least one hour between your starting point and your destination. You should never waste this time. The ability not to let this hour go to waste does not depend on your time management skills. Your ability to enjoy every minute of your life is a skill that needs practice, and practice, and practice again.

***

Time – a very simple word. It has only four letters. But everything in this world has its own time and sequence. Spring always comes after the winter, and autumn never comes before the summer.

Take the water drops that fall down from an icicle. They cannot form before the icicle is created by a wintry cold and the snow. Then they start dropping only after the icicle starts thawing, and the time of their journey through the air is short but it has direction.

People often believe that time can teach and heal, but that is not true. Time only separates the moments. Experience can teach people. Actions create experience. And the healing is done from within you. Time is needed for actions and for healing. Use your time wisely, because every second counts.

***

Every morning is a wonderful morning. The skies are bright and clear. Early birds are only just about to start singing. There is still a chill in the air and you begin to shiver a little after getting out from the warmth of your car. But it is not a problem; you know you will warm up once you start walking.

One last yawn and you start your way up to the top of a mountain that rises up to the sky. Your first task is to find a path that will lead you to the top. After that you will need to decide the pace of your walk. Walking too fast can be dangerous as you would tire quickly and can fall down and injure yourself, or worse still - fall off the cliff into abyss below. Walk too fast – and you won't be able to see much, because you will have to concentrate on the ground under your feet, you won't see the magnificent view of the mountain. Walking fast and looking down to the path you won't see the beautiful flowers that grow only in the mountains but nowhere else, nor you will see the glaciers that have not yet fully melted creating tiny transparent creeks that run down the hill. But there is a dilemma. If you go too slowly you will not have enough time to finish your walk before the sun goes down. So, choosing the right pace is as important as finding the path. At the end of the day, when you come back to your starting point and sit in your car glancing back to the mountain you realise what beautiful things you would have missed if you haven't left your comfort zone this morning but kept driving instead of taking that walk. You choose the right path and walked the right pace, having enough courage to complete your trip made you happy. People often try to make a choice between the path to pursue and the speed of going ahead in life. But different paths will lead to the different end points, and taking a slow or a fast pace will mean the quality of their life's walk. One needs to choose not between the two but both – the path AND the pace.

***

Another day another dollar, another day another squalor. Another morning came to me, another mug of coffee saved my life, again. Swearing like a sailor, I am starting to put my clothes on, while murmuring to myself:

- What this new day will bring into my life? Hope that it will be only the good news. I was working hard yesterday and the day before, so I fully deserve to be successful today.

Life is simple – you need to work hard and one day you will make your career. Life is difficult – you will not get your promotion without some luck. I have finished putting my clothes on. Now I am fully awake and ready to step out into the new day of my life. When the last dreams have faded out of my head I felt grateful for another day of my life. Grateful for the new opportunities that I will be facing today. And I am now ready to accept the truth is that happiness is not just one big ball of 'joy'. Happiness consists of a number of little happy moments. So I am fully ready to create these moments of happiness for myself. I wish to everyone to have more happy moments than sad moments. Probably this is the simplest recipe of a happy life – to have more happy moments than sad.

***

Abandoned buildings with empty rooms filled up with only dust. The rooms still remember the laughter of the people who once lived there. They watch you passing by, not giving them a second glance. Their pain of longing is silent and lonely.

Why have they been abandoned, now staying empty collecting only memories? What have they done to deserve that? Why were they left behind? Their dark empty windows are like the hollow eye sockets of a skull, watching life from the other side of the grave. Do you feel sorry for these abandoned buildings when you see them? Do you actually see them? I do. These empty buildings and their loneliness – all are the products of human irresponsibility. People have built them, neglected them and eventually abandoned.

When I see empty houses I feel sorry not for people who have once occupied those rooms but for the rooms, which trusted their owners and were betrayed by them.

***

Imagine – you are on the top of the hill overlooking a beautiful valley. It is a misty morning and valley is submerged in a thick fog. Everything is hidden – the grass, the trees, and a small creek that runs between the bushes...

You cannot see anything except the white mist moving slowly around your feet. But you know for sure that everything should be there even though you cannot see it because of the fog. If you close your eyes you can even see the clear picture of this valley with your mind's eye. You stand there motionless for a while, then glance at the dial of your wristwatch and start walking your way down the valley. You make your first step, unsure, not knowing whether the picture you hold in your mind is there for real. You still hesitate, and maybe a small fear creeps into your mind too. But despite feeling a bit scared you still go ahead, and after the first step you do the second, then the third, and the next one... You keep walking, going further and further into the mist. You are now on the move, well on your way to the valley. As you come closer the mist retreats. Step by step it draws back opening to your sight the green grass and the beautiful trees, you can hear the sounds of that hidden creek you have imagined now running somewhere ahead of you. You turn around and look back -

now, from the valley, you can see that the path you walked was much easier than you imagined it to be.

You take a deep breath and fill your lungs with clean fresh air; you can hear the birds singing in the trees' branches above your head. Now, you are confident and have decided to go ahead and find your way to the other side of the valley, to the farthest side that lies behind the creek. Maybe after this you will decide to go further, much further, even beyond the boundaries of the valley, who knows?

"I know. I make the decision."- You think to yourself. And you do know, indeed. Because you have overcome your fear and hesitation, you have made it down to the valley in the thick fog without a clear path laid before you. Now, after you walked through your fears and doubts, you realise that you always have to walk through the unknown, through the fog of uncertainty, before you reach your bright future.

Picture this: a river and a bridge, and nothing else around except a deserted field. Looks empty and lonely, doesn't it? Yes, it does look empty, and it is a still picture. But it is still only if you see them as inanimate things. Look carefully and the picture comes alive. The bridge stretches across the river that is running under it. It is a verb – stretches, the bridge is a living thing. It is also a verb – running. The river is also alive. There is a reflection of the bridge in the water, and the water running under the bridge sounds like a fresh and pure song. The picture is no longer still.

The picture is no longer lonely either. The River and the Bridge have got each other for company. The Bridge is a loyal friend to the River and is guarding it during long and cold winters when the River is asleep covered by the ice. This friendship is a long lasting one. The bridge is only there because of the river, people have built it. If the River will dry out, the Bridge will be demolished as well. Both the River and the Bridge know this but it doesn't matter, because they both know that the Bridge lives not for people, but for the River.

***

Sometimes I feel trapped. Sometimes I feel like the whole world is against me. Sometimes I feel empty as if somebody took my soul and all my hope out of my body. I guess, probably every person had experienced such kind of a feeling at least once in their life.

But when I feel this way, when I feel I am in a dark place, I try to remind myself there are a few simple things that are true.

Darkness is not a physical obstacle and is not the reason to give up on your chosen path. Some people will stay within their zone of comfort the whole life only because they are scared to follow a dark path. If I don't continue to go forward and stay put, then I will stay in darkness forever. There is no such darkness in this world that cannot be broken up by a flame of a single candle. After the darkness the light is so much brighter.

Dark times can come to everybody. Sometimes, just a smile from a stranger can break the darkness. Share your smile with those in darkness, and one day when you are in the dark, somebody else's smile will give you the support you so need, just as your smile had done it for others.

***

Get up in the middle of the night when it's still dark, get out of bed, and put your clothes on. Take a candle and some safety matches or a cigarette lighter, and go out. Find some quiet place away from the wind and light up the candle you took from home. After you done this, move about twenty feet back and look at the candle. What do you see? A light. The light is coming from the candle you left there. Even from afar the small candle light is visible in the darkness. You now can go back home and think of it no more, but you will remember this little light in the middle of the darkness for the rest of your life.

Love is a candle light inside your soul. But this candle was not lit up by you. This was done by another person who had entered a dark and quiet place in your heart, and ignited a candle of love in there. It is now up to you to keep it burning, shining bright, to protect from everything that could extinguish this warm flame.

Printed in Great Britain
by Amazon